Autism in the Family

Navigating the Challenges Together

Lester Dipas Laoagan

Ukiyoto Publishing

All global publishing rights are held by

Ukiyoto Publishing

Published in 2023

Content Copyright © Lester Dipas Laoagan

ISBN 9789367951255

All rights reserved.
No part of this publication may be reproduced,
transmitted, or stored in a retrieval system, in any
form by any means, electronic, mechanical,
photocopying, recording or otherwise, without the
prior permission of the publisher.

The moral rights of the author have been asserted.

This book is sold subject to the condition that it shall
not by way of trade or otherwise, be lent, resold, hired
out or otherwise circulated, without the publisher's
prior consent, in any form of binding or cover other
than that in which it is published.

www.ukiyoto.com

First and foremost I thank God because without him none of this is possible.
To my family for believing and supporting my writing journey.
For my brother Clarence

Contents

Understanding Autism Spectrum Disorder	1
What is Autism Spectrum Disorder?	2
Causes and risk factors	4
Common symptoms and characteristics	6
Diagnosis and assessment	8
Living with an Autistic Brother	11
Emotional impact on siblings	12
Challenges and opportunities	14
Differences in communication and social interaction	16
Dealing with sensory issues	18
Building a Support System	20
Family dynamics and roles	21
Finding resources and services	23
Working with healthcare providers and educators	25
or Sister, Parents and Caregivers, and Healthcare Professionals.	25
Advocacy and legal rights	27
Legal Protections	28
Resources	30
Tips for Effective Advocacy	31
Developing Positive Relationships	33
Strengthening sibling bonds	34
Here are some tips for strengthening sibling bonds:	35
Nurturing social skills and friendships	37
Encouraging independence and self-esteem	39
Managing conflicts and misunderstandings	41
Addressing Behavioral Issues	43

Understanding challenging behaviors	44
Strategies for prevention and intervention	46
Positive reinforcement and consequences	48
Working with therapists and specialists	50

Encouraging Learning and Development 52

Identifying strengths and interests	53
Adapting to different learning styles	55
Promoting academic success and vocational skills	58
Encouraging hobbies and creativity	60
Here are some tips to encourage hobbies and creativity in individuals with autism:	61

Planning for the Future 63

Transitioning to adulthood	64
Employment and independent living options	66
Estate planning and financial considerations	68
Dealing with loss and grief	70

Building a Brighter Future Together 73

Embracing diversity and inclusion	74
and Sister, Parents/Caregivers, and Educators.	74
Celebrating progress and achievements	76
Finding joy and meaning in the journey	78
Supporting each other through life's challenges.	80
Communication is Key	81
Be Patient	82
Celebrate Small Wins	83

About the Author   84

Understanding Autism Spectrum Disorder

What is Autism Spectrum Disorder?

Autism Spectrum Disorder (ASD) is a complex developmental disorder that affects the way an individual communicates, interacts with others, and perceives the world around them. It is called a spectrum disorder because the symptoms and severity can vary widely from person to person. Some individuals with ASD may have difficulty with social interactions and communication, while others may have repetitive behaviors or intense interests in specific topics.

ASD is typically diagnosed in early childhood, often around the age of two or three. However, some individuals may not receive a diagnosis until later in life. The cause of ASD is not fully understood, but research suggests that it is a combination of genetic and environmental factors.

The symptoms of ASD can range from mild to severe and may include:

- Difficulty with social interactions, such as making eye contact or understanding social cues

- Delayed language development or difficulty with verbal communication

- Repetitive behaviors or routines, such as lining up toys or flapping hands

- Intense interests in specific topics or objects

- Sensory sensitivities, such as being bothered by certain sounds or textures

It is important to note that not all individuals with ASD will have all of these symptoms, and some may have additional symptoms not listed here. Additionally, individuals with ASD may also have other conditions or challenges, such as ADHD or anxiety.

There is currently no cure for ASD, but early intervention and therapy can help individuals with ASD improve their communication and social skills, manage challenging behaviors, and lead fulfilling lives. Treatment may include speech therapy, occupational therapy, behavioral therapy, and medication for co-occurring conditions.

As a family member or caregiver of someone with ASD, it is important to educate yourself about the condition and seek support from professionals and other families in similar situations. With the right support and resources, individuals with ASD can thrive and live happy, fulfilling lives.

Causes and risk factors

The causes of autism are still not completely understood, but there are several factors that are believed to contribute to the development of the disorder. Some of these factors include genetics, environmental factors, and neurological factors.

Genetics plays a signicant role in the development of autism. Studies have shown that if one child in a family is diagnosed with autism, the chances of another child in the same family also having the disorder are much higher than in families without a history of autism. Researchers have identified numerous genes that are associated with autism, but it is believed that multiple genes are involved, each contributing to a small part of the disorder.

Environmental factors are also believed to play a role in the development of autism. Exposure to toxins such as lead and mercury during pregnancy or early childhood may increase the risk of developing autism. Viral infections during pregnancy or early childhood have also been linked to the development of autism.

Neurological factors are also believed to contribute to the development of autism. Studies have shown that children with autism have differences in brain structure and function compared to typically developing children. These differences may affect how the brain processes information, leading to the symptoms associated with autism.

Risk factors for autism include being male, having a sibling with autism, and having certain medical conditions such as Fragile X syndrome or tuberous sclerosis. Advanced parental age has also been linked to an increased risk of autism.

It is important to note that while these factors may contribute to the development of autism, they do not cause the disorder. Autism is a complex disorder that likely has multiple causes and risk factors.

Knowing the potential causes and risk factors for autism can help families understand the disorder and make informed decisions about their child's care. Early identification and intervention can greatly improve outcomes for children with autism, so it is important for families to seek help if they suspect their child may have the disorder.

Common symptoms and characteristics

Autism is a complex neurodevelopmental disorder that affects social, communication, and behavioral skills in individuals. It is a spectrum disorder, which means that symptoms and characteristics vary from one person to another. However, there are some common symptoms and characteristics that can help identify autism in individuals.

Social symptoms: One of the key characteristics of autism is difficulty in social interaction. Children with autism may struggle to make eye contact, initiate conversation, and understand social cues. They may also prefer to play alone or engage in repetitive behaviors instead of playing with other children.

Communication symptoms: Individuals with autism may have difficulty understanding and using language. They may not speak at all or have delayed speech development. They may also struggle with nonverbal communication such as gestures, facial expressions, and body language.

Behavioral symptoms: Repetitive and stereotypical behaviors are common in individuals with autism.

They may engage in repetitive movements such as rocking, spinning, or clapping their hands. They may also have obsessive interests or routines and become upset if their routine is disrupted.

Sensory symptoms: Many individuals with autism have sensory processing issues. They may be hypersensitive to certain sounds, textures, tastes, or smells. They may also be hypo-sensitive to sensory input and seek out sensory stimulation.

Other symptoms: Individuals with autism may also have other medical or mental health conditions such as seizures, anxiety, or ADHD. They may also have difficulty with motor skills such as coordination and balance.

It is important to note that not all individuals with autism will display these symptoms and characteristics, and that symptoms may present differently at different ages. If you suspect that a family member may have autism, it is important to seek a professional evaluation from a qualified healthcare provider or specialist in autism spectrum disorders. Early intervention and support can make a significant difference in the lives of individuals with autism and their families.

Diagnosis and assessment

Diagnosis and assessment are critical components of autism spectrum disorder (ASD) management. A formal diagnosis is essential in identifying the symptoms and determining appropriate treatment options. An early diagnosis can help families and caregivers to provide early intervention and support services to the individual with autism.

For parents, the initial diagnosis of their child with autism can be a challenging and emotional experience. However, it's important to remember that an early diagnosis provides an opportunity for the child to receive timely interventions. The assessment process typically involves a comprehensive evaluation by a team of professionals, including a pediatrician, a psychologist, a speech-language pathologist, and an occupational therapist.

During the assessment, the professionals will evaluate the child's strengths and weaknesses, communication and social skills, and behavior patterns. They will also consider the child's medical history and family history of autism. The assessment may take several weeks or months, depending on the severity of the symptoms and the availability of the professionals.

Once a formal diagnosis is confirmed, parents can work with the healthcare team to develop a comprehensive treatment plan. The treatment plan may include behavioral therapy, speech therapy, occupational therapy, and medication. The healthcare team will also provide guidance on how to manage the child's symptoms and behaviors at home.

For siblings of individuals with autism, the diagnosis and assessment process can be a confusing and overwhelming experience. It's important to involve the siblings in the process and provide them with age-appropriate information about autism. Siblings may benefit from counseling or support groups to help them understand and cope with their brother or sister's diagnosis.

For caregivers, the diagnosis and assessment process can help to guide their approach to care. Caregivers can work with the healthcare team to develop a personalized care plan that addresses the individual's unique needs and preferences. Caregivers may also benefit from support groups and educational resources to help them navigate the challenges of caring for an individual with autism.

In conclusion, the diagnosis and assessment process is critical in managing autism spectrum disorder. It provides families and caregivers with the information and resources they need to provide the best care and support to individuals with autism. With early intervention and ongoing support, individuals with autism can achieve their full potential and lead fulfilling lives.

Living with an Autistic Brother

Emotional impact on siblings

Sibling relationships are some of the most important and enduring relationships that we experience in our lifetime. They are often our first friends and confidants, and they play a vital role in shaping our emotional development. For siblings of children with autism, however, the emotional impact can be particularly challenging.

Siblings of children with autism often face unique challenges that can lead to feelings of isolation, frustration, and resentment. They may feel neglected or overlooked as their parents focus their attention on their autistic sibling. They may also struggle to understand and communicate with their sibling, who may have difficulty expressing themselves or engaging in social interactions.

These challenges can have a significant emotional impact on siblings, leading to feelings of anxiety, depression, and stress. They may also impact the sibling's social development, as they may struggle to form close relationships with peers or understand social cues and norms.

It is important for parents to recognize and address these emotional challenges. They can do this by creating opportunities for siblings to connect with others who are facing similar challenges, such as support groups or online communities. They can also encourage open communication and provide a safe space for siblings to express their feelings and concerns.

Parents can also work to involve siblings in the care and support of their autistic sibling. This can help them to develop a sense of purpose and connection, while also building their understanding and empathy for their sibling's condition.

Ultimately, it is important for parents to recognize the unique emotional challenges that siblings of children with autism face, and to provide the support and resources they need to navigate these challenges successfully. By doing so, they can help to build strong and enduring sibling relationships that will benefit the entire family for years to come.

Challenges and opportunities

Raising an autistic child can be challenging, but it can also be an opportunity to grow and learn as a family. Challenges come in many forms, from navigating the educational system to managing daily routines and behaviors. However, with the right support and resources, families can overcome these challenges and find opportunities for growth and connection.

One of the biggest challenges for families with an autistic child is navigating the educational system. Many parents struggle to find the right school or program for their child, and may not know how to advocate for their child's needs. This can be especially difficult if the child has complex needs or if the school is not equipped to provide the necessary support.

To overcome this challenge, it's important for families to educate themselves about the options available and to seek out support from advocacy groups and professionals. This can help parents become effective advocates for their child and ensure that they receive the education and support they need to thrive.

Another challenge families face is managing daily routines and behaviors. Autistic children often have difficulty with transitions and may become overwhelmed by sensory input. This can make it difficult to establish routines and to manage everyday tasks like getting dressed, eating, and going to bed.

To overcome this challenge, families can work with their child's therapist or other professionals to develop strategies for managing behaviors and establishing routines. This may involve creating visual schedules, using sensory tools like weighted blankets or fidget toys, and providing clear and consistent expectations for behavior.

Despite the challenges, there are also many opportunities for families with autistic children. These opportunities may include developing closer relationships with each other, learning new skills, and discovering new interests and passions.

For example, many families and that their child's autism opens up new avenues for creative expression and exploration. Autistic children may have unique talents and interests, such as a fascination with numbers or a passion for music. By supporting these interests, families can help their child develop a sense of purpose and identity.

Overall, raising an autistic child can be challenging, but it can also be a rewarding and enriching experience for families. By seeking out support and resources, families can overcome challenges and find opportunities for growth and connection.

Differences in communication and social interaction

As a family member of an autistic brother, it can be difficult to understand the differences in communication and social interaction that your sibling experiences. It is important to recognize that these differences are a fundamental aspect of autism and should be approached with empathy and understanding.

Communication differences can manifest in many ways, such as difficulty with verbal communication or challenges with nonverbal cues. Your sibling may struggle with initiating conversations, maintaining eye contact, or understanding sarcasm and figurative language. Additionally, they may have a preference for routine language and struggle with expressing their emotions.

Social interaction differences can also vary greatly among individuals with autism. Your sibling may have difficulty with understanding social cues and norms, struggle with initiating and maintaining friendships, or experience sensory overload in social situations. They may also have a preference for solitary activities, such as reading or playing video games.

It is important to note that these communication and social interaction differences are not a result of a lack of intelligence or effort on your sibling's part. Rather, they are a product of neurological differences that are characteristic of autism.

As a family member, it is important to approach your sibling's communication and social interactions with patience and understanding. You can help by using clear and direct language, avoiding sarcasm and figurative language, and providing visual aids or social stories to help them understand social norms and expectations.

You can also help by creating a supportive and inclusive environment for your sibling. This can include finding activities that they enjoy and feel comfortable with, providing opportunities for socialization in a low-pressure environment, and advocating for their needs in school or other settings.

Finally, it is important to remember that every individual with autism is unique and experiences communication and social interaction differences in their own way. By listening to your sibling, being patient and understanding, and providing support, you can help them navigate these challenges and thrive in their own way.

Dealing with sensory issues

Dealing with sensory issues can be one of the most challenging aspects of autism for both the autistic individual and their family members. Sensory processing difficulties can make it difficult for people with autism to tolerate certain sounds, textures, smells, or visual stimuli. This can greatly impact their daily life and cause them to avoid certain situations or become overwhelmed and anxious.

As a family member of an autistic individual, it's important to understand the sensory issues that they may be experiencing. This can involve observing their behavior and asking them about their experiences. It's also important to create a safe and supportive environment that accommodates their sensory needs.

One way to do this is by creating a sensory-friendly space in your home. This can involve using calming colors, minimizing clutter, and reducing harsh lighting. You can also provide sensory tools such as weighted blankets, fidget toys, or noise-cancelling headphones to help them cope with sensory overload.

It's also important to be mindful of the sensory environment when you're out in public. This can involve avoiding crowded or noisy places, or bringing along sensory tools to help them cope with sensory overload. It's also important to be patient and understanding if they need to take breaks or leave a situation that is overwhelming for them.

In addition to creating a sensory-friendly environment, there are also therapies and interventions that can help with sensory processing difficulties. Occupational therapy can help individuals develop coping strategies and improve their ability to process sensory information. Sensory integration therapy involves exposing individuals to different sensory experiences in a controlled environment to help them become more comfortable with sensory stimuli.

Dealing with sensory issues can be a challenging aspect of autism, but with the right support and understanding, individuals with autism can learn to navigate the sensory world more effectively. As a family member, it's important to be patient, understanding, and supportive in helping them manage their sensory needs.

Building a Support System

Family dynamics and roles

As life goes on, families evolve and adapt to different dynamics and roles. For families with an autistic brother, the dynamics and roles can be unique and challenging. The way each family member handles the situation can have a significant impact on the family's overall wellbeing.

In a family with an autistic brother, parents usually play a central role in providing care and support for their child. They may have to learn new skills and techniques to communicate and connect with their autistic child. At times, this can be overwhelming, and parents may need to seek outside help from professionals, such as therapists or special educators.

Siblings of an autistic brother may also play an essential role in the family dynamic. They may experience a mix of emotions, ranging from love and understanding to frustration and resentment. It is essential to create a supportive environment where siblings can discuss their feelings and concerns with their parents and other family members.

One of the significant challenges in families with an autistic brother is balancing the needs of the autistic child with the needs of other family members. It is essential to create a routine that works for everyone in the family, including the autistic brother. This routine should be flexible enough to accommodate the needs of the autistic brother while also allowing other family members to pursue their interests and activities.

Communication is a crucial factor in maintaining a healthy family dynamic. Family members should be encouraged to communicate openly and honestly with each other. It is essential to listen to each family member's concerns and feelings and work together to find solutions that work for everyone.

In conclusion, families with an autistic brother face unique challenges in maintaining a healthy family dynamic. However, with patience, understanding, and communication, families can navigate these challenges together and create a supportive and loving environment for everyone.

Finding resources and services

When someone in the family is diagnosed with autism, it is important to find resources and services that can help them navigate the challenges that come with this condition. As a family member, parent, or caregiver, you play a crucial role in ensuring that your loved one with autism receives the support they need to thrive.

One of the first steps in finding resources and services is to connect with local organizations that specialize in autism. These organizations can provide you with information about local support groups, therapy services, educational programs, and other resources that can help your loved one with autism. They may also be able to connect you with other families in similar situations, which can be a great source of support and advice.

Another important resource is your loved one's school or educational program. Schools are required to provide accommodations and support for students with disabilities, including autism. Talk to your loved one's teachers and school administrators about what services and accommodations are available, and work with them to develop an individualized education plan (IEP) that meets your loved one's needs.

Therapy services are also an important resource for families of individuals with autism. Applied behavior analysis (ABA) therapy is a common treatment for autism that focuses on behavior modification and skill-building. Other types of therapy that may be helpful include speech therapy, occupational therapy, and physical therapy.

In addition to these resources, there are many online resources that can provide you with information and support. Autism Speaks, the Autism Society of America, Autism Society Philippines and the National Autism Association are just a few examples of organizations that provide information, support, and advocacy for families of individuals with autism.

Overall, finding resources and services for your loved one with autism can be a daunting task, but it is essential for their well-being and success. By connecting with local organizations, schools, and therapy services, and utilizing online resources, you can ensure that your loved one with autism receives the support they need to thrive.

Working with healthcare providers and educators or Sister, Parents and Caregivers, and Healthcare Professionals

When it comes to caring for a loved one with autism, it can often feel like you're navigating a maze. There are so many different approaches to treatment and so many different people involved in the process. One of the most important groups of people you'll work with are healthcare providers and educators. These professionals can play a critical role in helping your loved one reach their full potential.

As a family member, it's important to start by building a strong relationship with your healthcare providers and educators. This means being open and honest about your loved one's needs and their progress. It also means listening carefully to the advice and recommendations of these professionals, even if you don't always agree with them.

One of the most important things you can do when working with healthcare providers and educators is to be an advocate for your loved one. This means speaking up when you feel that their needs are not being met, and working closely with these professionals to come up with solutions that work for your family.

Another key aspect of working with healthcare providers and educators is communication. You should always be open and transparent about your loved one's progress and any concerns you may have. This will help these professionals to better understand your loved one's needs and to provide more effective care.

Finally, it's important to remember that working with healthcare providers and educators is a partnership. You should be actively involved in your loved one's care, attending appointments and meetings, and staying informed about their progress. By working together, you can help your loved one to achieve their full potential and lead a happy, healthy life.

In conclusion, working with healthcare providers and educators is an essential part of caring for a loved one with autism. By building strong relationships, advocating for your loved one, communicating effectively, and working in partnership, you can help your loved one to thrive and achieve their full potential.

Advocacy and legal rights

As a family with an autistic brother, it is important to understand the legal rights and entitlements of individuals with autism. Advocacy is crucial in ensuring that your brother's rights are upheld, and that he receives the necessary support and accommodations. In this chapter, we'll explore some of the legal protections and resources available, as well as some tips for effective advocacy.

Legal Protections

The Americans with Disabilities Act (ADA) is a federal law that prohibits discrimination against individuals with disabilities, including autism. This law applies to many aspects of daily life, such as education, employment, and public accommodations. Under the ADA, your brother has the right to reasonable accommodations in these areas, such as extra time on tests, modified job duties, or accessible facilities. It is important to know that the ADA also covers harassment and bullying based on disability, which can be common issues for individuals with autism.

The primary law with respect to the rights of persons with disabilities in the Philippines is Republic Act (R.A.) No. 7277 or the Magna Carta for Disabled Persons – An act providing for the rehabilitation, self-development and self-reliance of persons with disabilities and their integration into the mainstream of society and for other purpose. The act was amended in 2006 by Republic Act No. 9442 – "An act providing for the Rehabilitation and Self-Reliance of Disabled Persons and Their Integration to the Mainstream of Society and Other Purposes granting Additional Privileges and Incentives and Prohibitions on Verbal, Non-Verbal Ridicule and Vilification Against Persons with Disability," which required the Department of Health (DOH) to institute a national health program for PWDs, establish medical rehabilitation centers in provincial hospitals and adopt an integrated and comprehensive approach to the health development of PWDs which shall make essential services available to them at affordable cost.

Another important law to be aware of is the Individuals with Disabilities Education Act (IDEA), which ensures that children with disabilities receive a free and appropriate public education. This law requires schools to provide individualized education plans (IEPs) for students with disabilities, which should outline specific goals, accommodations, and support services. As a family member, you have the right to be involved in the IEP process and to advocate for your brother's needs.

Resources

There are many resources available for families of individuals with autism, including legal advocates and disability rights organizations. The Autism Society of America is a national organization that provides information, support, and advocacy for individuals with autism and their families. Local disability rights organizations may also offer legal assistance and advocacy services.

Tips for Effective Advocacy

Advocacy can be a challenging and sometimes overwhelming process, but there are some tips that can help. Here are a few suggestions:

- Educate yourself: Understanding your brother's legal rights and entitlements is the first step in effective advocacy. Take time to research the laws and resources available, and don't be afraid to ask questions.

- Communicate clearly: When advocating for your brother, it's important to communicate clearly and effectively. Be specific about your concerns and needs, and provide evidence or documentation when possible.

- Build relationships: Building positive relationships with teachers, administrators, and other professionals can be helpful in advocating for your brother. Take the time to get to know these individuals and work collaboratively to find solutions.

- Don't give up: Advocacy can be a long and sometimes frustrating process, but don't give up. Keep pushing for the services and support that your brother needs, and remember that you are his strongest advocate.

In conclusion, understanding your brother's legal rights and entitlements is essential in advocating for him. By educating yourself, utilizing resources, and implementing effective advocacy strategies, you can help ensure that he receives the support and accommodations he needs to thrive.

Developing Positive Relationships

Strengthening sibling bonds

Strengthening Sibling Bonds

Having a sibling with autism can be a unique experience, and it can come with its own set of challenges. However, it can also be an incredibly rewarding and enriching experience for both the sibling with autism and their neurotypical siblings. Developing strong sibling bonds is essential for building a supportive and loving family dynamic.

Here are some tips for strengthening sibling bonds:

Encourage Communication: Communication is key to building strong relationships, and it is especially important when one sibling has autism. Encourage open and honest communication between siblings, and make sure that each sibling feels heard and validated.

2. Embrace Differences: Siblings with autism often have different needs and ways of communicating than their neurotypical siblings. It is important to embrace these differences and find ways to work together that accommodate everyone's needs.

3. Find Common Interests: Finding common interests can be a great way to bond with a sibling with autism. Whether it's a shared love of music, video games, or animals, finding something to enjoy together can help build a strong bond.

4. Foster Empathy: Empathy is a crucial skill for all siblings, but it is especially important when one sibling has autism. Encourage neurotypical siblings to try to understand their sibling's perspective and feelings.

5. Create a Safe Space: Siblings with autism may have sensory issues or other challenges that make certain

environments stressful for them. Creating a safe space where they can feel comfortable and relaxed can help build a strong bond between siblings.

6. Seek Support: It's important for both neurotypical and autistic siblings to have support outside of the family. Look for support groups or therapy options that can help siblings navigate the challenges of having a sibling with autism.

Building strong sibling bonds takes time and effort, but it is essential for creating a supportive and loving family dynamic. By embracing differences, fostering empathy, and finding common interests, siblings can build a bond that will last a lifetime.

Nurturing social skills and friendships

As a family member of an autistic brother, one of the most important things you can do is to nurture their social skills and friendships. Autism can make it difficult for individuals to understand social cues, initiate conversations, or maintain eye contact, which can make socializing and forming friendships a challenge. One of the best ways to help your autistic brother develop social skills is to provide them with opportunities to practice. Encourage them to participate in group activities, such as sports teams, clubs, or hobbies that they enjoy. This will help them to interact with others who share similar interests and develop social skills while having fun.

It is also important to teach your autistic brother appropriate social behavior. This can include teaching them how to initiate conversations, how to read body language, and how to maintain eye contact. Role-playing exercises can be a helpful tool in teaching social skills, as they allow your brother to practice various social scenarios in a safe environment.

Another effective way to help your autistic brother develop social skills is to work with their school or therapist to create a social skills group. These groups typically involve small groups of autistic individuals working together to practice social skills and form friendships. This can be a great way for your brother to interact with and learn from others who are facing similar challenges.

In addition to helping your autistic brother develop social skills, it is important to encourage and support their friendships. Autistic individuals may struggle with forming and maintaining friendships, but having close relationships can be incredibly beneficial for their mental health and wellbeing.

Encourage your brother to participate in activities with friends, such as going to the movies or playing video games together. Additionally, make an effort to support their friendships by inviting their friends over for dinner or hosting a playdate. This can help your brother feel more comfortable and confident in social situations and encourage the development of lasting friendships.

In conclusion, nurturing social skills and friendships is crucial for the wellbeing of individuals with autism. By providing opportunities to practice social skills, teaching appropriate social behavior, and encouraging friendships, you can help your autistic brother develop the skills and confidence they need to succeed socially.

Encouraging independence and self-esteem

Encouraging independence and self-esteem are crucial aspects of supporting individuals with autism. It is essential to understand that every individual with autism is unique and will have varying degrees of independence and self-esteem. For some, independence may mean being able to complete simple tasks, while for others, it may mean being able to live independently. Similarly, self-esteem may be affected by different factors such as social interactions, academic performance, and physical abilities.

Parents and siblings play a vital role in supporting their loved ones with autism to achieve independence and self-esteem. The first step is to recognize and acknowledge their strengths and abilities, rather than focusing on their weaknesses. This can be achieved by engaging in activities that they enjoy, such as sports, art, or music. Finding and nurturing their interests can help them build self-confidence and self-esteem.

Another way to encourage independence is by establishing routines and schedules. Individuals with autism thrive in structured environments, and having a routine can help them feel secure and in control of their lives. Parents and siblings can work together to create a schedule that includes daily activities such as waking up, eating, and going to bed. This will help them develop time management skills and a sense of responsibility.

Social skills are also an essential aspect of independence and self-esteem. Many individuals with autism struggle with social interactions, which can lead to isolation and low self-esteem. Parents and siblings can encourage social skills by providing opportunities to interact with others, such as joining clubs, participating in team sports, or volunteering. They can also work with their loved ones to develop social scripts and practice social situations in a safe and supportive environment.

Finally, it is essential to recognize that independence and self-esteem are not achieved overnight. It takes time, patience, and support to help individuals with autism develop these skills. It is important to celebrate even small achievements and to provide encouragement and positive feedback along the way.

In conclusion, encouraging independence and self-esteem is a crucial aspect of supporting individuals with autism. Parents and siblings can play a vital role in nurturing their loved ones' strengths and abilities, establishing routines and schedules, encouraging social skills, and providing positive feedback and encouragement. With the right support and guidance, individuals with autism can achieve their full potential and lead fulfilling lives.

Managing conflicts and misunderstandings

Managing conflicts and misunderstandings is a crucial aspect of living with autism in the family. Autism can impact the way individuals communicate and understand social cues, leading to misunderstandings and conflicts. However, it is essential to understand that conflicts and misunderstandings are a natural part of any family dynamic and not exclusive to autism.

One of the most important steps in managing conflicts and misunderstandings is to communicate effectively. Effective communication involves active listening, understanding the other person's perspective, and expressing oneself clearly. For families with autistic members, it may be necessary to adapt communication strategies to accommodate their unique needs. For example, using visual aids or social stories to help explain social situations can be beneficial.

Another crucial aspect of managing conflicts and misunderstandings in families with autism is to recognize when to seek outside help. This can include therapy, counseling, or support groups. It is essential to remember that seeking help is not a sign of weakness, but rather a proactive step towards improving family dynamics.

It is also crucial to understand that conflicts and misunderstandings can arise from the stress and challenges of living with autism. It is essential to prioritize self-care for all family members to prevent burnout and resentment. This can include taking breaks, practicing mindfulness, and seeking support from friends and family members.

Finally, it is essential to approach conflicts and misunderstandings with empathy and understanding. It can be challenging to navigate the complexities of autism, and it is essential to recognize that everyone is doing their best. By approaching conflicts and misunderstandings with patience and empathy, families can work through challenges and grow stronger together.

In conclusion, managing conflicts and misunderstandings is an important aspect of living with autism in the family. By prioritizing effective communication, seeking outside help when necessary, prioritizing self-care, and approaching conflicts with empathy, families can navigate the challenges of autism and grow stronger together.

Addressing Behavioral Issues

Understanding challenging behaviors

Understanding challenging behaviors is a critical aspect of supporting individuals with autism spectrum disorder (ASD). Challenging behaviors can include a wide range of actions, from tantrums and aggression to self-injury and property destruction. These behaviors can be frustrating and confusing for family members, but they are often a form of communication for individuals with ASD.

It is essential to remember that challenging behaviors are not intentional. Individuals with ASD have difficulty communicating and regulating their emotions, leading to frustration and stress. Challenging behaviors can be a response to environmental stressors, sensory overload, or an inability to express their needs verbally.

To understand challenging behaviors, it is essential to observe and document the behavior. This process can help identify patterns and triggers for the behavior. Family members can work with professionals, such as behavior analysts and therapists, to develop a behavior plan that includes strategies for preventing and responding to challenging behaviors.

Prevention strategies include creating a predictable and structured environment, providing sensory breaks, and teaching coping skills. Response strategies involve de-escalation techniques, such as removing the individual from the situation, using calming techniques, and providing comfort and support.

It is crucial to remember that challenging behaviors can also be an indication of other underlying issues, such as medical or mental health concerns. Family members should work with healthcare professionals to rule out any medical issues and provide appropriate treatment.

Overall, understanding challenging behaviors is critical to support individuals with ASD and improve their quality of life. By observing behavior, identifying triggers, and developing preventative and response strategies, family members can help reduce the frequency and intensity of challenging behaviors. It is essential to approach challenging behaviors with patience, empathy, and a willingness to learn and adapt.

Strategies for prevention and intervention

As a family with an autistic brother, it can be challenging to navigate the various obstacles that come with this unique situation. However, there are numerous strategies for both prevention and intervention that can help make daily life more manageable and enjoyable for everyone involved.

One critical prevention strategy is to create a routine for your autistic brother. Autistic individuals often thrive on predictability and structure, so establishing a consistent schedule can help reduce anxiety and prevent meltdowns. It's also essential to provide plenty of sensory stimulation and opportunities for exercise, as these activities can be calming and improve overall mood.

Another prevention strategy is to create a safe and secure home environment. This may include installing locks on doors and windows to prevent wandering or creating a calming space where your brother can retreat when feeling overwhelmed. It's also important to remove any potential hazards and provide ample supervision to ensure your brother's safety.

When it comes to intervention, there are various strategies you can employ to help your brother manage challenging behaviors. One effective technique is to use positive reinforcement, where you reward good behavior and ignore negative behavior. This can involve offering praise or tangible rewards, such as stickers or small toys, for completing tasks or exhibiting positive behaviors.

Another intervention strategy is to use visual supports, such as picture schedules or social stories, to help your brother understand expectations and better navigate social situations. You can also consider working with a therapist or counselor who specializes in autism to develop personalized interventions and strategies.

Finally, it's essential to prioritize self-care as a family. Caring for an autistic brother can be emotionally and physically exhausting, so taking time for yourself and seeking support from others can help prevent burnout and ensure that you are better equipped to provide the care and support your brother's needs.

In conclusion, there are numerous prevention and intervention strategies that can help families with an autistic brother navigate the challenges and enjoy a fulfilling life together. By creating routines, establishing a safe home environment, using positive reinforcement, and prioritizing self-care, you can help your brother thrive and improve the overall quality of life for your family as a whole.

Positive reinforcement and consequences

Positive reinforcement and consequences are two important concepts that parents and caregivers of autistic children must understand. Positive reinforcement involves rewarding good behavior to encourage its repetition, while consequences refer to the outcome of inappropriate behavior. Both of these concepts are important in shaping the behavior of autistic children and promoting their overall development.

Positive reinforcement is a powerful tool in shaping behavior. By providing a reward for good behavior, children are more likely to repeat the behavior. Rewards can be anything that is motivating to the child, such as praise, a favorite toy, or a special treat. It is important to identify what motivates your child and use that as a reward. Positive reinforcement should be applied consistently, so that the child is clear on what behaviors are being rewarded. Over time, the child will begin to associate the positive behavior with the reward and be more likely to repeat it.

Consequences are also an important part of shaping behavior. Inappropriate behavior should be met with consequences that are appropriate for the behavior.

Consequences can include time-outs, loss of privileges or toys, or a simple verbal reprimand. It is important to be consistent with consequences, so that the child understands what is expected of them. It is also important to provide clear explanations for why the behavior is inappropriate and what the consequences will be if it continues.

It is important to note that consequences should not be used as punishment. Punishment is not an effective way to shape behavior, as it often leads to resentment and resistance. Instead, consequences should be viewed as a natural outcome of inappropriate behavior.

By providing clear and consistent consequences, children will begin to understand the relationship between their behavior and the outcome.

In conclusion, positive reinforcement and consequences are important tools for shaping the behavior of autistic children. By providing rewards for good behavior and consequences for inappropriate behavior, parents and caregivers can promote positive development and help children become more independent and successful. It is important to be consistent and clear in applying these concepts, so that the child understands what is expected of them and can learn to make positive choices on their own.

Working with therapists and specialists

Working with therapists and specialists is an important aspect of supporting an autistic brother. These professionals have specialized knowledge and skills to help individuals with autism navigate the challenges they face in their daily lives. As a family member, it is important to understand how to work with therapists and specialists effectively to ensure the best outcomes for your brother.

One of the first things to consider when working with therapists and specialists is to find the right professional for your brother's needs. This may involve researching different professionals and their areas of expertise to find someone who can address your brother's specific challenges. It is also important to consider your brother's personality and preferences when choosing a therapist or specialist, as a good fit can greatly enhance the effectiveness of treatment.

Once you have identified a therapist or specialist, it is important to establish a collaborative relationship. This involves open communication, sharing information about your brother's strengths and challenges, and actively participating in the treatment process. As a family member, you can provide valuable insights into your brother's behavior and experiences, which can help the therapist or specialist develop effective interventions.

Another important aspect of working with therapists and specialists is to be consistent with treatment. This involves attending appointments regularly, following through with recommended interventions, and providing ongoing support to your brother. Consistency can help your brother develop trust and rapport with the therapist or specialist, which can positively impact the effectiveness of treatment.

It is also important to recognize that working with therapists and specialists is just one aspect of supporting an autistic brother. As a family, it is important to provide a supportive and accepting environment that encourages your brother's strengths and interests. This may involve adjusting family routines and activities to accommodate your brother's needs, or advocating for his rights and needs in school, social settings, and the community.

In summary, working with therapists and specialists can be a valuable tool for supporting an autistic brother, but it is important to approach this process collaboratively, consistently, and holistically. By working together as a family to support your brother's needs, you can help him thrive and navigate the challenges of autism with greater resilience and success.

Encouraging Learning and Development

Identifying strengths and interests

Identifying strengths and interests is a crucial step in understanding and supporting individuals on the autism spectrum. As a family member of an autistic brother, it is essential to recognize and appreciate their unique strengths and interests to help them thrive.

Autistic individuals often have a range of strengths and talents that are often overlooked due to their challenges with socialization and communication. Identifying these strengths can help families, educators, and therapists to develop individualized support plans that cater to their strengths and interests.

One way to identify strengths is to observe and take note of activities and tasks that the individual enjoys and excels in. For instance, an autistic individual might have a talent for playing musical instruments or possess remarkable abilities in mathematics. It is also essential to recognize the repetitive behaviors that the individual engages in as they can be indicators of their interests.

Another way to identify strengths is to conduct assessments that measure the individual's cognitive abilities, academic strengths, and interests. Assessments such as the Cognitive Assessment System

(CAS) can help to identify a range of cognitive abilities, including memory, perception, and reasoning. The Strong Interest Inventory can help to identify career interests and skills.

It is also important to note that not all autistic individuals have the same strengths and interests. Therefore, taking an individualized approach is crucial to identify and support their unique strengths.

Once strengths and interests are identified, it is important to provide opportunities for the individual to develop and showcase their skills. This can be through specialized classes or programs, hobbies, or volunteering activities that align with their interests. It is also crucial to provide support in areas where the individual may struggle, such as socialization or communication.

In conclusion, identifying strengths and interests is an essential step in supporting autistic individuals. Recognizing their unique talents and providing opportunities to develop and showcase them can help them thrive and lead fulfilling lives. As a family member of an autistic brother, taking an individualized approach and appreciating their strengths and interests can help strengthen your relationship and improve their quality of life.

Adapting to different learning styles

Understanding different learning styles is essential when it comes to teaching and supporting individuals with autism. Every person has unique strengths and weaknesses in the way they learn, process information, and understand the world around them. As a family member of an autistic brother, you need to be aware of his learning style and adapt your teaching and communication methods accordingly. Here are some tips for adapting to different learning styles:

Visual Learners

Many individuals with autism are visual learners, which means they learn best through pictures, diagrams, and visual aids. They may struggle to process spoken language and rely on visual cues to understand the meaning of words. If your brother is a visual learner, you can use visual aids such as picture books, videos, or diagrams to help him understand concepts and ideas. You can also use color coding, labeling, and visual schedules to help him organize his thoughts and activities.

Auditory Learners

Some individuals with autism are auditory learners, which means they learn best through spoken language and sound. They may have a keen sense of hearing and be able to pick up on subtle sounds and nuances in language. If your brother is an auditory learner, you can use spoken language, music, and sound effects to help him learn and remember information. You can also use repetition and verbal cues to reinforce key concepts and ideas.

Kinesthetic Learners

Kinesthetic learners learn best through hands-on experiences and physical activities. They may struggle to sit still and focus on verbal instruction or written materials. If your brother is a kinesthetic learner, you can engage him in physical activities such as sports, games, or art projects to help him learn and express himself. You can also use hands-on materials such as toys, puzzles, or manipulatives to help him understand concepts and ideas.

Multimodal Learners

Some individuals with autism are multimodal learners, which means they have a combination of learning styles. They may learn best through a combination of visual, auditory, and kinesthetic experiences. If your brother is a multimodal learner, you can use a variety of teaching methods and materials to help him learn and understand information. You can also encourage him to use his strengths in different areas to support his learning in other areas.

In conclusion, adapting to different learning styles is crucial for supporting individuals with autism. As a family member, you can play a vital role in identifying your brother's learning style and adapting your teaching and communication methods accordingly. By doing so, you can help him reach his full potential and navigate the challenges of autism together.

Promoting academic success and vocational skills

Promoting academic success and vocational skills is crucial for individuals on the autism spectrum to lead a fulfilling life. It is essential to recognize the unique strengths, interests, and challenges of each individual to provide them with the best opportunities to succeed.

Academic success can be achieved through various approaches, including individualized education plans (IEPs), accommodations, and modifications. IEPs are personalized plans developed by the school with input from the family and professionals to address the child's specific needs. Accommodations and modifications can be provided to help the child learn in their preferred way, such as visual aids, sensory tools, and technology.

It is also crucial to promote vocational skills to help individuals on the autism spectrum transition into adulthood successfully. Vocational skills refer to the abilities needed to perform a job, such as communication, time management, problem-solving, and social skills. These skills can be developed through vocational training programs, internships, and job coaching.

Families can support their autistic siblings by encouraging their interests and hobbies, which can lead to the development of vocational skills. For instance, if the sibling enjoys cooking, they can learn culinary skills and pursue a career in the food industry. It is also vital to provide opportunities for socialization and community involvement, such as volunteering and participating in clubs and organizations.

Moreover, families can collaborate with schools, community organizations, and professionals to create a network of support for their autistic siblings. This network can provide resources, guidance, and opportunities for academic and vocational success.

In conclusion, promoting academic success and vocational skills is essential for individuals on the autism spectrum to achieve their potential and lead a fulfilling life. By recognizing their unique strengths and challenges, providing individualized support, and encouraging their interests, families can help their autistic siblings succeed academically and vocationally.

Encouraging hobbies and creativity

Hobbies and creativity are essential for everyone, including individuals on the autism spectrum. They not only provide a sense of purpose and fulfillment but also allow people to express themselves freely. Encouraging hobbies and creativity in individuals with autism can help them in many ways, including improving social skills, reducing stress and anxiety, and enhancing cognitive abilities.

As a family member of an autistic brother, it is important to understand their interests and provide them with opportunities to explore their passions. It is essential to be patient and supportive while introducing new hobbies and activities. It may take some time for them to develop an interest, but once they do, it can be a great source of joy and fulfillment.

Here are some tips to encourage hobbies and creativity in individuals with autism:

Observe and Listen: Observe your brother's interests and listen to their preferences. This can help you understand what activities they might enjoy and what they may not be interested in.

2. Start Small: Start with small activities that are easy to understand and do not require a lot of time or commitment. For example, if your brother likes drawing, start with a basic drawing class or simple coloring books.

3. Provide Resources: Provide the necessary resources for their hobbies or creative activities. For example, if your brother enjoys painting, provide him with the necessary tools such as paint, brushes, and canvas.

4. Join a Group: Encourage your brother to join a group or club related to their interests. This can help them meet new people and develop social skills.

5. Be Positive and Encouraging: Encourage your brother to pursue their interests and be positive about their progress. This can help build their confidence and motivate them to continue. In conclusion, encouraging hobbies and creativity in individuals with autism can be

a great way to improve their wellbeing and quality of life. As a family member, it is important to support and encourage their interests, be patient, and provide the necessary resources. With the right support and encouragement, your brother can develop skills, find joy, and explore their passions.

Planning for the Future

Transitioning to adulthood

Transitioning to adulthood is a significant milestone for every individual, and it is especially crucial for individuals on the autism spectrum. The transition period can be a challenging time for autistic individuals and their families as it involves many changes, including transitioning from high school to college or the workforce, living independently, and navigating social relationships.

For parents of autistic individuals, the transition period can be an emotional rollercoaster. It is essential to plan and prepare for the transition to ensure that the individual with autism has the necessary tools and resources to achieve their goals and live a fulfilling life.

For siblings of autistic individuals, the transition period can also be challenging. It is essential to understand and support your sibling during this period, as they may feel overwhelmed and anxious about the changes that are occurring.

One of the critical aspects of transitioning to adulthood for individuals with autism is developing self-advocacy skills. Self-advocacy skills involve the ability to communicate one's needs, preferences, and goals effectively. It is crucial for individuals with autism to develop these skills to ensure that they can advocate for themselves in various settings, including the workplace, college, and social situations.

Another important aspect of transitioning to adulthood for individuals with autism is financial planning. It is essential to work with a financial planner to ensure that the individual with autism has the necessary resources to support themselves in the future. This can include setting up a trust or creating a budget to manage expenses.

Transitioning to adulthood for individuals with autism can also involve developing independent living skills. This can include learning how to cook, clean, and manage finances. It is essential to work with a therapist or counselor to develop these skills gradually.

In conclusion, transitioning to adulthood for individuals with autism can be a daunting task, but with proper planning and support, it can be a successful and fulfilling experience. It is essential to understand and support your loved ones during this period and work together to ensure that they have the necessary resources to achieve their goals and live a happy and fulfilling life.

Employment and independent living options

One of the biggest concerns for parents of children with autism is their child's future. As children with autism grow up, parents often worry about what life will look like for them as adults. Two major factors that contribute to the quality of life for adults with autism are employment and independent living.

Employment can be a challenge for individuals with autism. However, with the right support, many individuals with autism can lead successful careers. It is important to identify the strengths and interests of the individual and match them to a career that aligns with those strengths and interests. Additionally, it is important to provide the individual with the necessary supports to be successful in their chosen career. This may include job coaching, accommodations in the workplace, and ongoing training and support.

Independent living is also a concern for parents of children with autism. Many individuals with autism will require some level of support throughout their lives, but with the right supports, they can live independently. It is important to start planning for independent living early on. This may include teaching life skills such as cooking, cleaning, and managing finances. It may also involve identifying housing options that provide the necessary supports for the individual to live independently.

There are a variety of housing options available for individuals with autism. These include group homes, shared living arrangements, and independent living with support. It is important to consider the individual's preferences and needs when selecting a housing option. Additionally, it is important to consider the level of support that will be provided and the cost of the housing option.

Overall, employment and independent living options are important considerations for individuals with autism and their families. With the right supports, individuals with autism can lead successful careers and live independently. It is important to start planning for these options early on and to consider the individual's strengths, interests, and needs when making decisions.

Estate planning and financial considerations

Estate planning and financial considerations are essential for families with autistic brothers. The planning process can be complex and intimidating, but it is crucial to ensure that your loved one with autism is protected and provided for in the future.

One of the first steps in estate planning is creating a will or trust. This legal document outlines how you want your assets to be distributed after your death. It is essential to leave clear instructions on how your autistic brother should be provided for in your absence.

Another important consideration is guardianship. As your autistic brother approaches adulthood, you may need to establish legal guardianship to make decisions on his behalf. It is essential to discuss this process with an attorney to ensure that you choose the right guardian and understand your legal responsibilities.

Financial planning is also critical for families with autistic brothers. Many individuals with autism require specialized therapy, medication, and other support services, which can be expensive. It is essential to create a financial plan that includes funding for these services and other expenses related to your brother's care.

One option to consider is special needs trusts. These trusts are designed to provide financial support to individuals with disabilities while still allowing them to receive government benefits. Special needs trusts can be used to pay for medical expenses, education, housing, and other essential living expenses.

Finally, it is essential to consider your brother's long-term care needs. Many individuals with autism require ongoing care and support, which can be challenging to provide as they age. It is essential to plan for your brother's long-term care needs and consider options such as trustworthy relatives or friends, assisted living or group homes.

In conclusion, estate planning and financial considerations are critical for families with autistic brothers. It is essential to create a plan that protects your brother's interests and provides for his care and support in the future. By working with an attorney and financial planner, you can ensure that your brother's needs are met and that he has a secure financial future.

Dealing with loss and grief

For families with an autistic member, loss and grief can come in many forms. It may be the loss of a loved one, a pet, a job, a friendship, or even a routine. Whatever the cause, it can be challenging to navigate these emotions, especially when supporting an autistic brother or sibling. Here are some strategies that may help your family cope with loss and grief.

1.   Acknowledge the emotions.

It's essential to recognize and validate the emotions that come with loss and grief. This includes allowing each family member to express their feelings without judgment. For individuals with autism, this may mean using visual aids or social stories to help them understand and express their emotions.

2.   Maintain routines.

While it may be tempting to disrupt routines during times of grief, maintaining a sense of structure and predictability can be calming for individuals with autism. Try to keep regular activities and schedules as consistent as possible.

3. Seek support.

It's okay to ask for help during times of loss and grief. Reach out to friends, family, or a therapist for support. Additionally, there are many support groups and resources available specifically for families with autism.

4. Engage in self-care.

Taking care of yourself is essential during times of grief. This can include activities like exercise, meditation, or spending time in nature. It's important to prioritize self-care to avoid burnout and support your ability to care for your autistic brother or sibling.

5. Celebrate the memories.

Remembering and celebrating the memories of the person, pet, or routine that was lost can be healing for the entire family. This may include creating a memory book, planting a tree or garden, or participating in a charity event in their honor.

In conclusion, dealing with loss and grief can be challenging for any family, but it can be especially difficult when caring for an autistic sibling. By acknowledging emotions, maintaining routines, seeking support, engaging in self-care, and celebrating memories, families can navigate these challenges together. Remember that grief is a process, and each family member may need different levels and types of support.

Building a Brighter Future Together

Embracing diversity and inclusion and Sister, Parents/Caregivers, and Educators.

Embracing diversity and inclusion is essential when it comes to autism in the family. Autism is a neurodevelopmental disorder that affects individuals in different ways. It is essential to understand that people with autism are diverse and have unique strengths, challenges, and perspectives. Therefore, it is important to embrace and celebrate this diversity in our families, schools, and communities.

As a family member of someone with autism, it is important to be open minded and accepting of their differences. This means acknowledging and respecting their unique needs, interests, and abilities. It also means being patient and understanding when they struggle with social communication, sensory processing, or other challenges. By embracing diversity, we can create a positive and inclusive environment for everyone in the family.

Parents and caregivers can also play a critical role in promoting diversity and inclusion for their child with autism. One way to do this is by advocating for their child's needs and ensuring they receive the support and accommodations they require. This may involve working with educators, therapists, and other professionals to create a personalized plan that meets their child's unique needs. It is also essential to encourage and celebrate their child's strengths and talents, no matter how different they may be.

Educators can also contribute to embracing diversity and inclusion in the classroom. This means creating a welcoming and inclusive environment that values and respects all students. It also means providing accommodations and support to students with autism to ensure they have equal access to education. Educators can also incorporate inclusive teaching strategies and materials that celebrate diversity and promote understanding and acceptance.

In conclusion, embracing diversity and inclusion is crucial when it comes to autism in the family. By celebrating and valuing the unique strengths, challenges, and perspectives of individuals with autism, we can create a positive and inclusive environment for everyone. As family members, parents, caregivers, and educators, we have a responsibility to promote diversity and inclusion and ensure that everyone feels valued and respected.

Celebrating progress and achievements

Celebrating progress and achievements is an essential aspect of supporting individuals with autism and their families. It can be challenging to navigate the obstacles that come with autism, but it is important to acknowledge and celebrate the progress and achievements along the way. It provides a sense of hope, motivation, and encouragement to continue working towards the goals that have been set.

As a family member of an autistic brother or sister, it is crucial to recognize the progress and achievements that have been made, no matter how small they may seem. Celebrating progress could be as simple as acknowledging a new skill learned, a new word spoken, or a new friend made. It is essential to remember that progress is not always linear, and setbacks may occur. However, focusing on the progress made instead of the setbacks can help to keep a positive outlook.

Achievements can come in different forms, and it is crucial to understand that every individual with autism is unique. Celebrating achievements could be as simple as getting through a challenging day, finishing a new task, or participating in a new activity. Every individual with autism has their strengths and abilities, and it is important to acknowledge and celebrate these achievements, no matter how small they may be.

Celebrating progress and achievements not only benefits the individual with autism but also the family members. It helps to create a positive and supportive environment, which is essential for the overall well-being of the family. It also helps to build self-esteem, confidence, and a sense of accomplishment in the individual with autism.

In conclusion, celebrating progress and achievements is an essential aspect of supporting individuals with autism and their families. It is important to recognize and celebrate the progress and achievements no matter how small they may seem. It provides a sense of hope, motivation, and encouragement to continue working towards the goals that have been set. Celebrating progress and achievements is not only beneficial to the individual with autism but also to the family members. It helps to create a positive and supportive environment, which is essential for the overall wellbeing of the family.

Finding joy and meaning in the journey

As a family with an autistic brother, life can be challenging at times. You may feel overwhelmed, frustrated, and even hopeless. However, it's important to remember that despite the difficulties that come with autism, there are still many moments of joy and meaning to be found in this journey.

One of the first steps in finding joy and meaning is to focus on your brother's strengths and abilities. While it's easy to focus on the things he struggles with, take some time to identify the things he excels at. Maybe he has a talent for drawing, a great memory for facts, or a love of music. By focusing on these strengths, you can help your brother feel more confident and capable, which can lead to a greater sense of joy and purpose.

Another way to find joy and meaning in this journey is to focus on the small victories. It's easy to get caught up in the big picture and feel discouraged when progress seems slow. But by celebrating the small victories, you can stay motivated and find joy in the progress your brother is making. Maybe he learned a new word, made a new friend, or tried a new food.

These may seem like small things, but they are important milestones that should be celebrated.

Finally, it's important to take care of yourself and find joy in your own life. It's easy to get so caught up in caring for your brother that you forget about your own needs and desires. But by taking time for yourself and pursuing your own passions, you can find joy and meaning outside of your brother's autism. Maybe you enjoy playing a sport, reading, or spending time with friends. Whatever it is, make sure to prioritize your own happiness and wellbeing.

In conclusion, finding joy and meaning in the journey of having an autistic brother is possible. By focusing on his strengths, celebrating the small victories, and taking care of yourself, you can find joy and purpose in this journey. Remember, while there may be challenges along the way, there are still many moments of joy and meaning to be found.

Supporting each other through life's challenges

Supporting each other through life's challenges is a crucial aspect of family life, especially when one member is diagnosed with autism. It is important to understand that autism is a complex condition that affects individuals differently. As a family member of an autistic brother, you may find yourself struggling to cope with the challenges that come with the diagnosis. However, it is essential to remember that you are not alone in this journey. Here are some tips on how you can support each other through life's challenges. Create a Support System The first step in supporting each other is to create a support system. This system can include family members, friends, therapists, and support groups. Having a support system in place will help you to cope with the challenges that come with autism. It is essential to reach out to others who understand what you are going through and can offer support and advice.

Communication is Key

Communication is essential in any relationship, and it is especially important in a family where one member has autism. Be open and honest with each other about your feelings, needs, and concerns. Don't be afraid to ask for help when you need it, and be willing to offer support to your family members when they need it.

Be Patient

Autism can be challenging to deal with, and it requires a lot of patience. Be patient with your brother and other family members who may be struggling to cope with the diagnosis. Understand that it takes time to adjust to the changes that come with autism, and be willing to give each other time and space to process and adapt.

Celebrate Small Wins

Autism can make it difficult to achieve milestones, but it is essential to celebrate every achievement, no matter how small. Celebrating small wins can help to boost morale and encourage your brother to continue to work towards his goals. It can also help to create a positive environment where everyone feels supported and encouraged. In conclusion, supporting each other through life's challenges is essential in any family, but it is even more critical when one member is diagnosed with autism. Creating a support system, communicating openly, being patient, and celebrating small wins are all essential steps in supporting each other through the challenges that come with autism. Remember that you are not alone in this journey, and with the right support, you can navigate the challenges together.

About the Author

Lester D. Laoagan

Lester D. Laoagan is well aware about the challenges families with an autistic member or a member with autism. He is the author of The Man Without Personality, a biographical fiction based on the life of his autistic brother and how his family coped with their situation in the real world.

www.ingramcontent.com/pod-product-compliance
Lightning Source LLC
LaVergne TN
LVHW041538070526
838199LV00046B/1732